The children went to the park. They went with Mum and Dad.

They went to the stream.

Chip saw a rope. It was by a tree.

Dad had an idea.
"We can skip," he said.

He tied the rope to the tree.

Dad and the children began to skip.
"Go on, jump!" said Mum.

"Jump! Jump! Jump!"

They all jumped. They jumped
too soon.

Whoops! They all fell over.

Mum had an idea.

"Let's have a tug of war," she said.

Dad threw the rope over
the stream.

Mum went over the bridge.

The children began to pull.

Mum and Dad began to pull.

"Easy," said Wilf, and he let go.

Mum and Dad pulled and pulled.

"Easy," said Wilma, and she let go.

Mum and Dad pulled and pulled.

"Easy," said Biff and Chip, and
they let go.

"Pull, Dad!" called Wilma.

"Easy," said Kipper. "Look at me."

He pulled Mum and Dad into
the stream.

"Easy," said the man.